D0210942

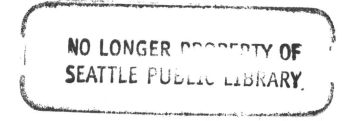

Katy Duck
Meets the Babysitter

By Alyssa Satin Capucilli   Illustrated by Henry Cole

Ready-to-Read

Simon Spotlight

New York   London   Toronto   Sydney   New Delhi

For Benjamin, with best wishes for
imaginative adventures, always. . . .
—A. S. C.

To miz mac, babysitter of yore
—H. C.

SIMON SPOTLIGHT
An imprint of Simon & Schuster Children's Publishing Division
1230 Avenue of the Americas, New York, New York 10020
Text copyright © 2012 by Alyssa Satin Capucilli
Illustrations copyright © 2012 by Henry Cole
For information about special discounts for bulk purchases, please contact Simon & Schuster
Special Sales at 1-866-506-1949 or business@simonandschuster.com.
The Simon & Schuster Speakers Bureau can bring authors to your live event. For more information or
to book an event contact the Simon & Schuster Speakers Bureau at 1-866-248-3049 or visit our website
at www.simonspeakers.com.
Manufactured in the United States of America 0712 LAK
First Edition
10 9 8 7 6 5 4 3 2 1
Library of Congress Cataloging-in-Publication Data
Capucilli, Alyssa Satin, 1957-
Katy Duck meets the babysitter / by Alyssa Satin Capucilli ; illustrated by Henry Cole. — 1st ed.
p. cm. — (Ready-to-read)
Summary: Katy Duck is unhappy about staying home when her parents go to a party, but her
babysitter's bag full of scarves provides a lot of fun.
[etc.]
[1. Babysitters—Fiction. 2. Scarves—Fiction. 3. Ducks—Fiction.] I. Cole, Henry, 1955- ill. II. Title.
PZ7.C179Kas 2012
[E]—dc23
2011042053
ISBN 978-1-4424-5241-1 (pbk)
ISBN 978-1-4424-5242-8 (hc)
ISBN 978-1-4424-5244-2 (eBook)

Mr. and Mrs. Duck
were getting dressed.
Katy Duck whirled
and twirled.

"Tra-la-la. Quack! Quack!
I want to go to the
party too," said Katy.

"You will have fun
with the babysitter, Katy,"
said Mrs. Duck.
"Here she is now."

"Tra-la-la. Quack! Boo!"
said Katy Duck.
"A babysitter is not
as much fun as a party."

Mr. and Mrs. Duck
gave Katy a big kiss.
"We will be back soon,"
they called.

"My name is Mrs. Duncan," said the babysitter. "You must be Katy Duck."

Katy looked right.

Katy looked left.

Katy looked Mrs. Duncan
up and down.

Mrs. Duncan wore
a fancy hat.
She held a
big, big bag.

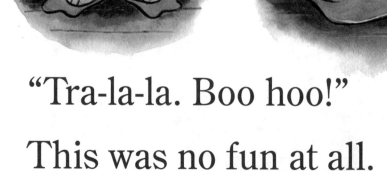

"Tra-la-la. Boo hoo!"
This was no fun at all.

"Come along, Katy,"
said Mrs. Duncan.
"Will you help me open
my bag?"

Katy Duck opened the
big bag. She peeked inside.
"It is filled with scarves!"
said Katy Duck.

"Why, these are not just scarves," said Mrs. Duncan. "This is a kite!"

She ran here. She ran there.

"How I love to fly a kite!

Do you want to try, Katy?"

"Tra-la-la. Quack! Hm-m-m."

That did look like fun.

Katy ran here.

She twirled there.

Mrs. Duncan chose
another scarf.
She bent. She swayed.
"Can you hear the wind?"

Katy bent. She swayed.
"Whoosh, whoosh, whoosh,"
called Katy. "I can hear
the wind. I can!"

"Look at me," said
Mrs. Duncan.
"I am an ocean wave."

"Look at me," said
Katy Duck.
"I am a bird.
Tra-la-la. Flap! Flap!"

Katy and the babysitter
danced and danced.

Soon Katy Duck was tired.

"Tra-la-la. Quack! Yawn!"

Mrs. Duncan tucked
Katy into bed.
She read a story.
She gave Katy a big hug, too.

"I did not know that
babysitters love to dance,"
said Katy Duck.
"Will you come again?"

"I would love to,"
said Mrs. Duncan.
"Sweet dreams, Katy Duck."

"Tra-la-la. Quack! Quack!" said Katy Duck.

"How I love my babysitter!"